For Helena, Natalia, and Nico
—P.D.J & J.S.

For Frank Thomas, Johnny, and Scarlet
—D.Y.

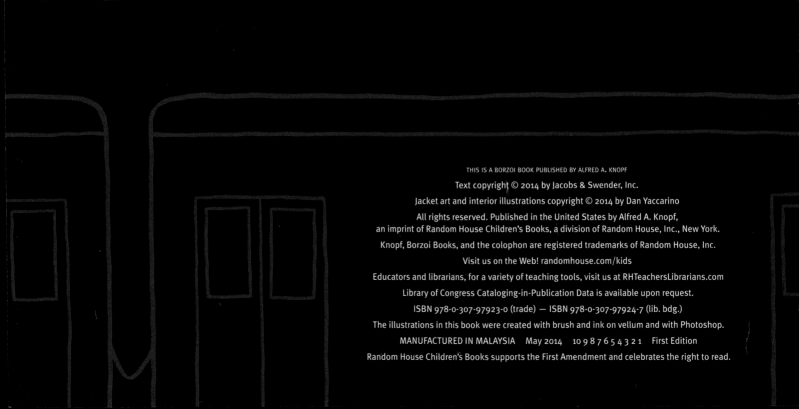

THIS IS A BORZOI BOOK PUBLISHED BY ALFRED A. KNOPF

Text copyright © 2014 by Jacobs & Swender, Inc.

Jacket art and interior illustrations copyright © 2014 by Dan Yaccarino

All rights reserved. Published in the United States by Alfred A. Knopf,
an imprint of Random House Children's Books, a division of Random House, Inc., New York.

Knopf, Borzoi Books, and the colophon are registered trademarks of Random House, Inc.

Visit us on the Web! randomhouse.com/kids

Educators and librarians, for a variety of teaching tools, visit us at RHTeachersLibrarians.com

Library of Congress Cataloging-in-Publication Data is available upon request.

ISBN 978-0-307-97923-0 (trade) — ISBN 978-0-307-97924-7 (lib. bdg.)

The illustrations in this book were created with brush and ink on vellum and with Photoshop.

MANUFACTURED IN MALAYSIA   May 2014   10 9 8 7 6 5 4 3 2 1   First Edition

Random House Children's Books supports the First Amendment and celebrates the right to read.

COUNT ON THE SUBWAY

by **Paul DuBois Jacobs**
& **Jennifer Swender**
illustrated by **Dan Yaccarino**

Alfred A. Knopf New York

1 MetroCard,

Momma and me.

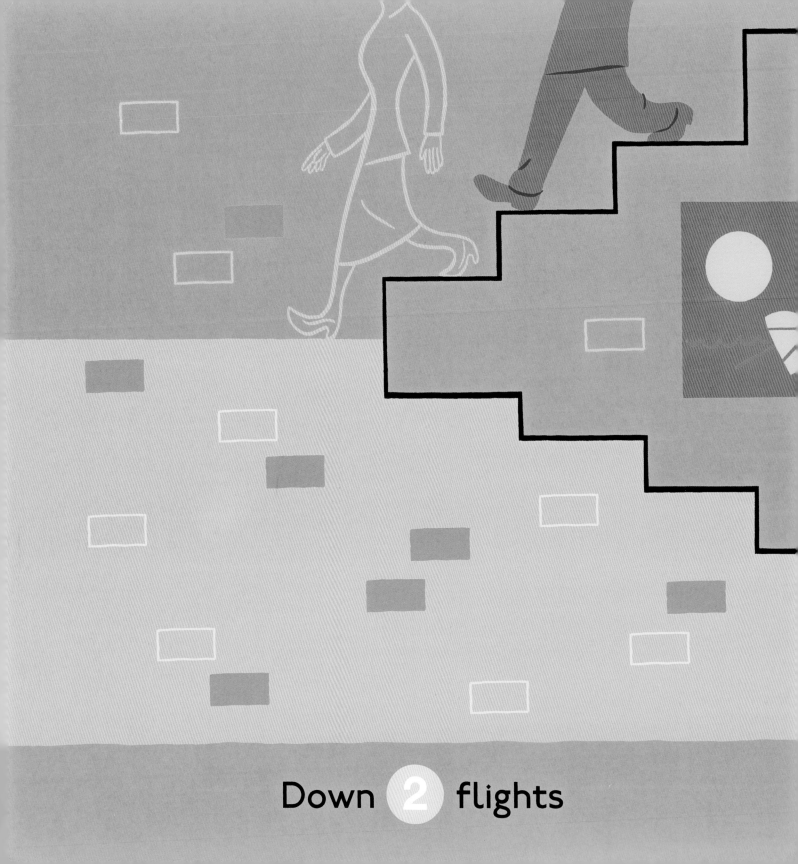

Down **2** flights

to catch the 3.

4 turnstiles, singers 5 .

A rumble, a screech, the train arrives.

6 empty seats, sit right down.

7 more stops, going uptown.

Big Apple subway, **8** cars long.

9 people off,
10 people on.

10 friends sway, boogie and bop

to a tunnel beat. . . . Here's our stop!

9 bright signs, down **8** stairs.

Find the **7** at Times Square.

6 straphangers stand their ground.

5 short minutes to cross town.

4 doors open. Time to move.

3 drums thumpin'
a rush-hour
groove.

2 escalators, up and down.

We arrive from underground.

1 station, central and grand.

Momma and me, hand in hand.